what time i

IT'S DUFFY TIME!

Audrey & Don Wood

SCHOLASTIC INC.

This book was originally published in hardcover by The Blue Sky Press in 2012.

ISBN 978-0-545-22097-2

12 11 10 9 8 7 6 5 4 3 2 1 14 15 16 17 18 19/0

Printed in the U.S.A. 40

First Scholastic paperback printing, March 2014

Duffy dedicates this book to his veterinarian,
Dr. Alan Nagakura

OH NO!

Duffy overslept!

The air smells like breakfast.

Duffy races into the kitchen
and asks for a bite to eat.

“Not yet,” his mistress says.
“It’s time to go out and potty.”
So Duffy does.

Waiting at the door
in the warm sunshine makes
Duffy sleepy, so he takes his
BEFORE BREAKFAST nap.

Breakfast at last! Duffy gobbles every bite.
He even licks the floor to make sure
he doesn't leave a crumb.

Because his tummy feels round and full,
Duffy knows it's time for his
AFTER BREAKFAST nap.

“Wake up, Duffy!” his mistress calls.
“We’ve got business to do.
Where’s your pirate hat?”

The line at the bank
is long, but at least
Duffy gets a
biscuit.

On the ride back
Duffy is exhausted.
He curls up for his
LATE MORNING nap.

It is good to be home. Duffy can't resist taking a quick MID-DAY nap in his comfy chair. The MID-DAY nap goes so well,

Duffy sleeps straight through
into his EARLY AFTERNOON nap.
A long nap makes for the best dreams.

"Duffeeeey!" a voice calls. His best friend is home

from school, and that means it's . . . Duffy time!

He wants to play longer,
but his best friend has
homework to do.
Duffy helps.

Something good is cooking in the kitchen.
Duffy asks for a nibble, but his food isn't ready,
so he takes his BEFORE DINNER nap, in a place
where no one will forget to feed him.

After dinner, the family goes
for a walk in the park.

Duffy enjoys sniffing trees
and saying hello to his friends.

Oh no!
Back at home, the master has stolen Duffy's comfy chair, but he squeezes in his Early Evening nap anyway.

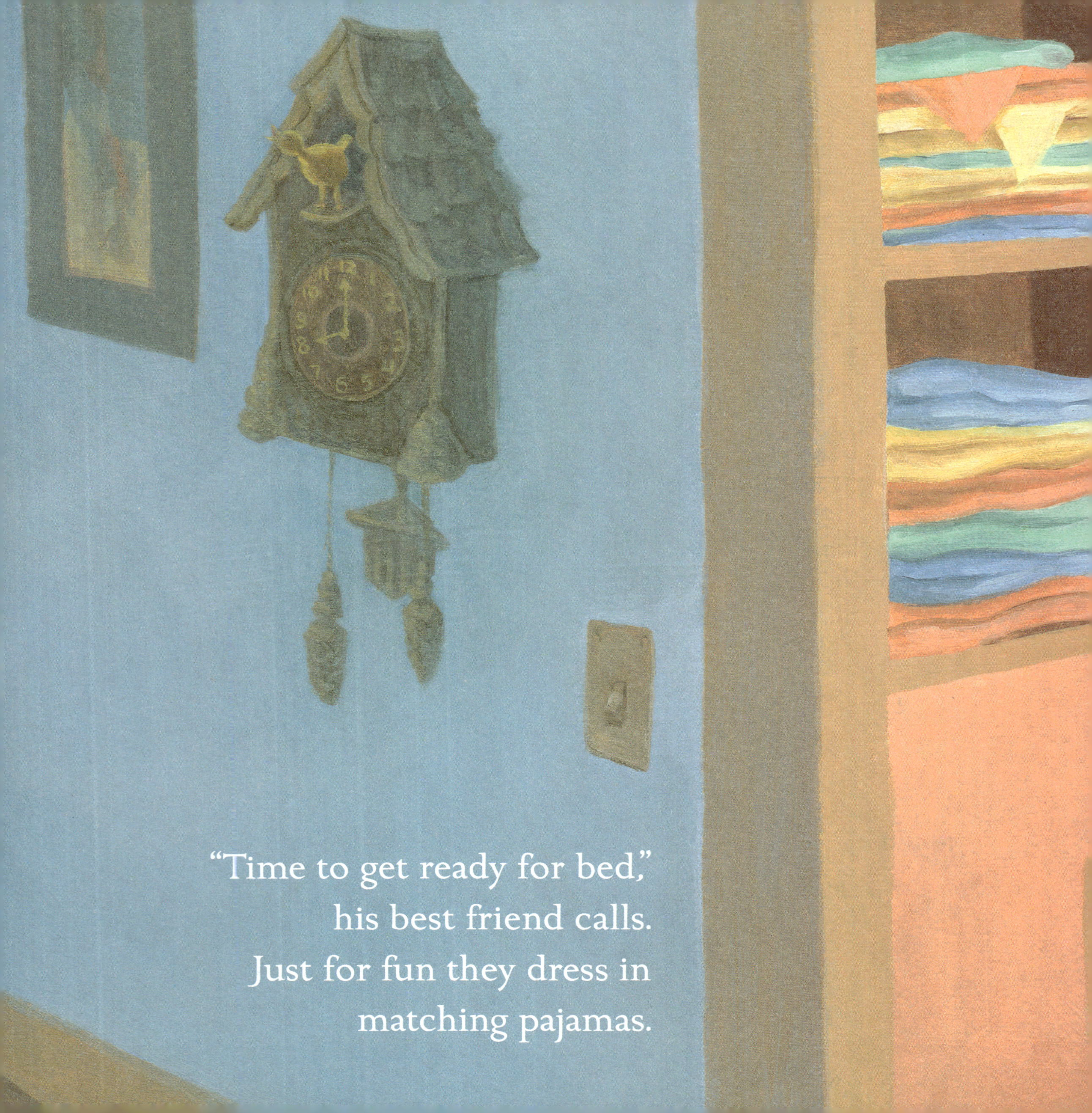

“Time to get ready for bed,”
his best friend calls.
Just for fun they dress in
matching pajamas.

There's nothing better than having your
best friend read you a good book at bedtime.
Duffy snuggles down and sighs with pleasure.
He doesn't feel sleepy at all.